To: _Brittany_

"The Lord is not slow to keep his promise" (2 Peter 3:9).

From: _Granny_

God's Promises for Girls
Copyright 1998 by The Zondervan Corporation
ISBN 0-310-975565

Published by

Zonderkidz™

The Children's Group of ZondervanPublishingHouse
Grand Rapids, Michigan 49530
A Division of HarperCollins Publishers
http://www.zonderkidz.com

Senior Editor: Gwen Ellis
Project Editor: Sarah Hupp
Creative Director: Patti Matthews
Art Design: Jane Dippold Design

Printed in China

98 99 00 /HK/ 3 2 1

God's Promises for Girls

The Lord Bless You & Keep You. *Numbers 6:24*

Wow! What a Wonderful Change!

You've changed so much from the time you were born. As a baby, you wiggled all the time. Your skin was wrinkly. And you even had trouble keeping your eyes open. But now you've changed into a little girl who can sit still for a while. You have a beautiful smile and a soft heart. And the twinkle in your eye shows just what you're feeling.

You've grown taller and stronger too. It's easier for you to do so many things for yourself. It wasn't very long ago that you didn't know how to dress yourself or how to use a spoon. But now you do both without even thinking twice.

You've learned so many things—how to tell the difference between a *b* and a *d,* how to ride a bike, how to write your name, and even how to blow bubbles in your milk. And you've learned how to be a friend and care about other people too. What a wonder you are!

Yet even before your friends and family ever knew you, God knew all about you. Before you were born, God knew you and loved you. That's hard to imagine. But it's true. The Bible says so.

"I know your name. I know all about you. And I am pleased with you."

Exodus 33:12

Before you were born I set you apart to serve me.

Jeremiah 1:5

"The Lord knows who his own people are."

2 Timothy 2:19

Before I was born the LORD chose me to serve him. He appointed me by name.

Isaiah 49:1

Your eyes saw my body even before it was formed. You planned how many days I would live. You wrote down the number of them in your book before I had lived through even one of them.

Psalm 139:16

I know my sheep, and my sheep know me.

John 10:14

Those who love God are known by God.

1 Corinthians 8:3

I know what you are doing. I know your love and your faith. I know how well you have served. I know you don't give up easily. In fact, you are doing more now than you did at first.

Revelation 2:19

My sheep listen to my voice. I know them, and they follow me.

John 10:27

He will sing with joy because of you.

Zephaniah 3:17

He will cover you with his wings.

Psalm 91:4

I am sure that the One who began a good work in you will carry it on until it is completed.

Philippians 1:6

God's Spirit lives in you.

1 Corinthians 3:16

God Loves You

God loves you! He loved you when you were a little baby, and he
loves you now too. God's love was big enough to love you when
you were little. And God's love will be big enough to love you
even when you are all grown-up. God's love is so big you will
never outgrow it.

God's love can't be broken either. His love is strong. In fact,
God's love is so strong, you can't pull away from it. His love is like
a superglue that glues your heart to his. And there's no way to
break the glue of God's love.

But best of all, God's love is full of forgiveness. God's love is
so forgiving that there's nothing you can do to make him stop loving you. Sometimes you may do bad things. You may say something mean to someone. You may get angry. But God will still
love you no matter what. God's love for you will never change!

"I have loved you with a love that lasts forever. I have kept on loving you with faithful love."

Jeremiah 31:3

The Lord's love for those who have respect for him lasts for ever and ever.

Psalm 103:17

We love because he loved us first.

1 John 4:19

I want you to realize that the Lord your God is God. He is the faithful God. He keeps his covenant for all time to come. He keeps it with those who love him and obey his commands. He shows them his love.

Deuteronomy 7:9

How great is the love the Father has given us so freely!

1 John 3:1

God loves us deeply. He is full of mercy.

Ephesians 2:4

Here is how God has shown his love for us. While we were still sinners, Christ died for us.

Romans 5:8

May you know his love, even though it can't be known completely. Then you will be filled with everything God has for you.

Ephesians 3:19

Nothing at all can ever separate us from God's love because of what Christ Jesus our Lord has done.

Romans 8:39

Jesus said: "The Father himself loves you because you have loved me."

John 16:27

The mountains might shake. The hills might be removed. But my faithful love for you will never be shaken.

Isaiah 54:10

My love for you is so strong it won't let you go.

Song of Songs 8:6

You are worth more than many sparrows.

Matthew 10:31

You're Special

Have you ever looked up at the clouds in the sky? Sometimes the clouds are white and fluffy. They pile on top of each other and look like scoops of ice cream. Sometimes the clouds are thin and long. They look like hair blowing in the wind. Sometimes the clouds are gray and full of rain. They may hide lightning and thunder. They may hide rushing winds. Yet God made each cloud. Each cloud is special. And each cloud is in the sky for a reason.

In a way, you are like the clouds. God made you, just the way you are. You may be tall. You may be short. You may have big feet. You may have small hands. You may have red hair or green eyes. You may even have freckles. But God made you, just the way you are. You are special to him. And you are special to other people. In fact, this world would not be complete without you in it!

The LORD is God. He made us, and we belong to him.
We are his people.

Psalm 100:3

You created the deepest parts of my being. You put me together inside my mother's body. How you made me is amazing and wonderful. I praise you for that. What you have done is wonderful. I know that very well.

Psalm 139:13–14

God created human beings in his own likeness. He created them in the likeness of God.

Genesis 1:27

I will take good care of you even when your hair is gray. I have made you. And I will carry you. I will take care of you. And I will save you. I am the Lord.

Isaiah 46:4

Lord, you have seen what is in my heart. You know all about me. You know when I sit down and when I get up. You know what I'm thinking even though you are far away . . . You know exactly how I live.

Psalm 139:1–3

LORD, you are our Father. We are the clay. You are the potter. Your hands made all of us.

Isaiah 64:8

Before I formed you in your mother's body I chose you. Before you were born I set you apart to serve me.

Jeremiah 1:5

I made you. I formed you when you were born.

Isaiah 44:2

LORD, you know me and see me. You test my thoughts about you.

Jeremiah 12:3

You are priceless to me. I love you and honor you.

Isaiah 43:4

God made us. He created us to belong to Christ Jesus. Now we can do good things.

Ephesians 2:10

Everything God created is good.

1 Timothy 4:4

God Cares About You

A mother duck and her six babies tried to cross a busy road. The mother duck started across the road first. The cars stopped to let the ducks go across. But halfway across the road, the last little baby stopped. The mother duck quacked at the baby. But the baby wouldn't move.

So the mother duck kept quacking. And while she was quacking, she pushed the five other babies quickly across the road. When the sixth baby still would not come, the mother duck went back into the road. She hurried up to the last baby duck and pushed him toward the grass along the roadside. The mother duck kept pushing him along until he was safe too.

God cares about you just like the mother duck cared about her babies. God watches over you every day. He knows what you need. He hears you when you pray. And God is so strong and so good that he will take care of you. That's a promise!

The Lord will command his angels to take good care of you.

Psalm 91:11

Turn all your worries over to him. He cares about you.

1 Peter 5:7

The angel of the Lord stands guard around those who have respect for him. And he saves them.

Psalm 34:7

"Because my people love me, I will save them. I will keep them safe, because they trust in me. They will call out to me, and I will answer them. I will be with them in times of trouble."

Psalm 91:14–15

Turn your worries over to the Lord. He will keep you going. He will never let godly people fall.

Psalm 55:22

The Lord's eyes look with favor on those who are godly. His ears are open to their prayers.

1 Peter 3:12

The LORD is good. When people are in trouble, they can go to him for safety. He takes good care of those who trust in him.

Nahum 1:7

The LORD is my shepherd. He gives me everything I need.

Psalm 23:1

From the time I was born, you took good care of me. Ever since I came out of my mother's body, you have been my God.

Psalm 22:10

Through faith you are kept safe by God's power.

1 Peter 1:5

I know that the LORD is always with me. He is at my right hand. I will always be secure.

Psalm 16:8

The LORD your God is God. He is the faithful God. He keeps his covenant . . . with those who love him and obey his commands. He shows them his love.

Deuteronomy 7:9

Fear Not!

Being afraid is not fun. Sometimes it seems that there are lots of things to be afraid of. Bad dreams can wake you up at night. New places can seem strange. You may be afraid of getting lost. New people can sometimes make you feel afraid too. You may be afraid of forgetting their names. You may be afraid of how they look, what they say, or how they dress.

Sometimes you may be afraid of being left alone. You may not want your parents to leave you with a new babysitter. You may not want your friends to go home. It may be so quiet when you are alone that you can hear strange noises. When no one is there to tell you what those noises mean, that can make you feel afraid.

God understands how you feel when you are afraid. He knows the things that scare you. But God wants you to know that he is always there. And God wants to give you special gifts that will help you when you are scared. He wants to give you peace. He wants to give you courage. He wants to give you faith.

I looked to the LORD, and he answered me. He saved me from everything I was afraid of.

Psalm 34:4

"I leave my peace with you. I give my peace to you. . . . Do not let your hearts be troubled. And do not be afraid."

John 14:27

"The Lord himself will go ahead of you. He will be with you. He will never leave you. He'll never desert you. So don't be afraid. Don't lose hope."

Deuteronomy 31:8

"Do not be afraid. I will set you free. I will send for you by name. You belong to me. You will pass through deep waters. But I will be with you. You will pass through the rivers. But their waters will not sweep over you. You will walk through fire. But you will not be burned. The flames will not harm you. I am the Lord your God. I am the Holy One. . . . I am the one who saves you."

Isaiah 43:1–3

When I'm afraid, I will trust in you.

Psalm 56:3

"Do not let your hearts be troubled. Trust in God. Trust in me also."

John 14:1

God didn't give us a spirit that makes us weak and fearful. He gave us a spirit that gives us power and love.

2 Timothy 1:7

You are the one who saves us. We will trust in you. Then we won't be afraid. LORD, you give us strength.

Isaiah 12:2

God is our place of safety. He gives us strength. He is always there to help us in times of trouble.

Psalm 46:1

Do not be afraid. I am with you. I will bless you.

Genesis 26:24

Even though I walk through the darkest valley, I will not be afraid. You are with me.

Psalm 23:4

Nearer Than a Best Friend

It's always fun to have friends to play with. It's fun to have a friend who likes to do the same things that you do. And best friends are the most fun of all. Best friends can share secrets. Best friends can play for hours without fighting. And best friends sometimes even know what you're thinking just by the way you look at them.

But best friends can't always be together. Sometimes best friends have to go home for supper. Sometimes best friends have to go away on vacation. And sometimes, best friends have to move away. That can make you feel lonesome. That can make you feel sad.

But God is a friend who will never move away. He wants to be your friend too. He already knows all about you. He already knows what makes you feel afraid. He loves you and cares about you. And God even knows what you're thinking about without even having to talk to you or look at you.

You never have to feel lonesome. God is always near. You never have to feel that you have no friends. God wants to be the best friend you've ever had.

Friends love at all times. They are there to help when trouble comes.

Proverbs 17:17

"I will ask the Father. And he will give you another Friend to help you and to be with you forever. The Friend is the Spirit of truth. . . . He lives with you, and he will be in you. I will not leave you like children who don't have parents. I will come to you."

John 14:16–18

Two people are better than one. They can help each other in everything they do. Suppose someone falls down. Then a friend can help him up.

Ecclesiastes 4:9–10

"I have called you friends. I have told you everything I learned from my Father."

John 15:15

Love each other deeply, from the heart.

I Peter 1:22

May the Lord make your love grow. . . . May your love for one another increase.

I Thessalonians 3:12

Dear friends, now we are children of God. He still hasn't let us know what we will be. But we know that when Christ appears, we will be like him.

1 John 3:2

Most of all, love one another deeply. Love erases many sins by forgiving them.

1 Peter 4:8

"Choose for yourselves right now whom you will serve. . . . As for me and my family, we will serve the LORD."

Joshua 24:15

"You are my friends if you do what I command. I do not call you servants anymore. . . . Instead, I have called you friends."

John 15:14–15

There is a friend who sticks closer than a brother or sister.

Proverbs 18:24

What Should You Choose?

When you were a little baby, you couldn't make any choices. Someone had to make all of them for you. Now that you're growing older, you can make some choices. You can choose which crayon to use when you color a picture. You can choose what games you want to play. You can even decide which friends you want to play with. Sometimes you can choose what you want to wear. You may even be able to choose which kind of vegetable you want to have for supper.

As you grow up, you will have even more choices to make. Those choices may be about how you should act. You will have to choose what you should say. You will have to make choices about where you should go. You will have to choose who should be your friends. You may be able to choose which school you want to go to. You may even have to choose where you want to live. Those choices will be very important.

Making choices isn't always easy. But God wants you to make good choices. He wants you to be wise. Making good choices will make you happy. Making good choices will make others happy too. And making good choices will please God.

"I am the Lord your God. I teach you what is best for
you. I direct you in the way you should go."

Isaiah 48:17

Trust in the LORD with all your heart. Do not depend on your own understanding. In all your ways remember him. Then he will make your paths smooth and straight.

Proverbs 3:5–6

If any of you need wisdom, ask God for it. He will give it to you. God gives freely to everyone.

James 1:5

Lord, I know that people don't control their own lives. They don't direct their own steps.

Jeremiah 10:23

Those who trust in themselves are foolish. But those who live wisely are kept safe.

Proverbs 28:26

A Promise Especially for You

There is a story in the Bible about a little boy who gave his lunch to Jesus. It was only a few pieces of bread and some fish. But the little boy gave Jesus all of his lunch. He didn't keep anything for himself. Jesus thanked God for the little boy's gift. And Jesus was able to share that lunch with a lot of people. It was a miracle.

The Bible tells us that God gave us something, too. He gave us his son, Jesus. He let Jesus die on a cross to wipe away all of our sins. That way everyone who believes in Jesus can be saved and go to heaven when they die. That's a miracle too.

The Bible says that you can give God something special. God wants you to give him your life. God wants you to trust him every day. He wants to be your friend. He wants to help you make wise choices. But most of all, God wants you to know that you can be forgiven for every bad thing you have ever done. When you give your life to God, a miracle will happen. You will have a changed heart. You will love God more. You will know you are forgiven. And that's the best promise of all.

"God loved the world so much that he gave his one and only Son. Anyone who believes in him will not die but will have eternal life."

John 3:16

Say with your mouth, "Jesus is Lord." Believe in your heart that God raised him from the dead. Then you will be saved.

Romans 10:9

Commit your life to the Lord. Here is what he will do if you trust in him. He will make your godly ways shine like the dawn. He will make your honest life shine like the sun at noon.

Psalm 37:5–6

Dear Jesus, I accept all of your promises for me.

(Your name)_____(Date)_____